THE BRILLIANT
DIAMOND JONES

When I finish reading, only Lenni and Tina clap.

"If you win the contest, are you going to split the money with us?" Alex asks with narrowed eyes.

Tina jumps in. "I liked the count, but you didn't describe the other characters as much."

"Yeah," Gaby says, looking hurt. "All Gabriela did was bring in food and follow her brother around."

"While Rob was the hero," Jamal says. "That figures."

I stand in the warm spotlight, my sweaty fingers clutching the typed pages. I thought the team would like seeing themselves in my story. Didn't they like anything about it?

ALIAS
DIAMOND JONES

CHRISTINA SALAT

Illustrations by Phil Franke

A CHILDREN'S TELEVISION WORKSHOP BOOK

BANTAM BOOKS
NEW YORK • TORONTO • LONDON • SYDNEY AUCKLAND

ALIAS DIAMOND JONES

A Bantam Book / October 1993

Ghostwriter, **Ghost writer** and ● are
trademarks of Children's Television Workshop.
All rights reserved. Used under authorization.
Art direction by Marva Martin
Cover design by Susan Herr
Interior illustrations by Phil Franke

ISBN 0-553-37216-5

Published simultaneously in the United States and Canada

Bantam Books are published by Bantam Books, a division of Bantam
Doubleday Dell Publishing Group, Inc. Its trademark, consisting of the
words "Bantam Books" and the portrayal of a rooster, is registered in
U.S. Patent and Trademark Office and in other countries. Marca Regis-
trada. Bantam Books, 1540 Broadway, New York, New York 10036.

OPM   0   9 8 7 6 5 4 3 2

CONTENTS

DEAR READER,

I HOPE YOU WILL GRAB A PEN AND SOME
PAPER AND EXPLORE YOUR WORLD AS ROB
EXPLORES HIS. THIS IS HOW FAMOUS
WRITERS BEGIN . . .

GHOSTWRITER

SCHOOL'S OUT!

RINGGGGGGGGGGGG!

"Yes!" Jamal Jenkins turns around in his seat and holds up his hand. We slap palms, high-five style, as a happy roar fills the school.

I grab my book bag.

"Have a good summer, people," Mr. Crew calls as everyone storms out of the room. "See you in the eighth grade!"

Jamal and I squeeze through the doorway into the crowded hall. I smile to myself. I, Rob Baker, have lived through another year at a new school.

The crowd sweeps us along, toward the school's front entrance. "I have to grab something out of my locker," I shout to Jamal. "Meet you out front."

I push through to my locker and open it one last time. My black-and-white postcards of writers are already untaped from

the back of the locker door and in a pile, waiting on the empty shelf. I take a notebook out of my book bag and carefully place Walter Dean Myers, C. S. Lewis, Ursula Le Guin, and the rest of them inside. Then I grab my skateboard and head out.

Lenni Frazier and Alex Fernandez are on the front steps, leaning against the railing with Jamal, when I come out.

"Hey, Rob! You survived your first year at Hurston," Lenni teases.

I nod. That's no joke. Starting over is not fun, though I guess I should be used to it by now.

We jump down the cement steps and I get on my board.

Alex, Jamal, and Lenni start walking. I whiz along beside them. The air never tasted so good. It's summer!

"I'm going to have the best time," Lenni says. She reaches up to pull the loose red bow from her brown hair. "My dad is renting studio time with his band and he said I could watch them record as soon as school is out." She gathers her hair and refastens it into a neat ponytail.

"Good deal," Jamal says. "Maybe they'll let you record one of your songs."

"Well, I've got a part-time summer job," Alex boasts.

"Doing what?" Lenni asks.

"My folks are going to pay me and Gaby to help out more at the store," he explains. "There's plenty I'd rather be doing than stacking fruit, but I'll have my own money." He rubs his

hands together happily. "I'm going to see every single movie that comes out, and play video games . . ."

"Personally," Jamal says, "all I'm going to do this summer is enjoy myself." He runs ahead of us a few steps, dribbling a pretend basketball. "I'm going to play some hoops . . ." He leaps up to make a shot and then crouches low. "And practice karate . . ."

Lenni looks at me. "What are you doing, Rob?"

I shrug. I don't have any summer plans. Usually my brother Jason comes home and we hang out, but this summer he's going to Germany with some kids from his school. Suddenly, two and a half months with nothing to do seems like a very long time.

The four of us stop by Washington Elementary School. Alex's sister Gaby spots us and runs over, pulling her friend Tina Nguyen along.

"Hi, team." Tina grins. "Who wants to come over to my house? I got this great new Vietnamese game. It's for mystery-solvers." She glances at Alex.

Gaby snickers. Everyone knows Tina and Alex like each other.

"I'm there," Alex says.

"Cool!" Lenni grins.

I shake my head. "I'm heading home."

Tina and the others look at me, surprised.

"Later," I say. I'm just not in the mood to hang right now. Giving a strong push with my left foot, I zoom away.

I let myself into the apartment on Dekalb Avenue where my folks and I have lived for the last year and walk into the bright, empty kitchen. A large brown envelope is on the table with Mom's handwriting scribbled across the front.

Rob, this came in the mail for you today. I'm at the gallery till at least 7 P.M. There's ravioli in the freezer and tomato sauce in the fridge for you & Dad. Don't wait on dinner if you're hungry.

The envelope is from Jason. Maybe he's coming home after all! I tear the package open. Inside is a thick, spiral-bound book with a small yellow note stuck to the cover.

June 16
Hi, Buddy! I found this at a bookstore and knew it was meant for you. Hope you'll dedicate your first novel to me!
Sorry I won't be in Brooklyn this summer, but I'll send postcards from every castle I visit and you'd better let me know what's up with you, too. Have fun.
Miss ya. Love, Jason.

I peel the note off the book. *Writer's Truths* is stenciled in gold script across the soft black cover. In bold letters on the first page it reads:

The only way to be a writer is to write.

So he isn't coming home. I close the book and set it down on the kitchen table, trying not to feel disappointed. It's a cool gift. But I wish Jason were here. What am I going to do by myself all summer?

I reach into the cupboard above the sink for a glass and pour myself some cold fruit punch. Sitting down at the round table, I pick up the book again. It feels solid and promising. I flick through the crisp, blank pages. I've been writing stories since I was little. I've never had anything published, but that's always been my dream.

I open the book to its first lined page. At the top, it says,

**The way to start something is to begin.
WHAT IN YOUR LIFE WOULD YOU LIKE TO BEGIN?**

Hmmm. I unzip the front pocket of my book bag and take out a pen. Suddenly I see a glow of light sweeping over the bold black letters, making them shimmer. I smile. Ghostwriter!

Ghostwriter is . . . well, he's hard to explain. But he's very cool. He contacted me one day when I was working on the computer at school. Not many people can see his writing—just me, Jamal, Lenni, Alex, Gaby, and Tina. He writes to us, and we write to him. We're the Ghostwriter team.

The words on the page pulse slightly, glowing the question at me.

WHAT IN YOUR LIFE WOULD YOU LIKE TO BEGIN?

I uncap the pen and begin to write.

When anyone asks what I want to be when I grow up, I know the answer. I've always wanted to be a writer, with my books on library shelves and my articles in magazines. But I tell people "I don't know."

Letters scramble on the page. A single word forms.
WHY?

I don't know. . . . I'm thirteen, so no one bugs me about it much, except my dad. He wouldn't think "writer" is a good answer. He knew he wanted to be a military man when he was my age and he did something about it right after he finished high school.

I'm scared to tell people my dream, in case I can't make it come true. My two desk drawers are full of poems, short stories, and plays. I think I'm a good writer, but I don't know if I'm good enough.

I want to write stuff that gets bought and published. I could be proud of that.

YOU CAN BE PROUD NOW, Ghostwriter writes. YOU ARE A FINE WRITER.

Ghostwriter's words make me feel good, but I'm talking about something different. Something big.

I chew on my pen, thinking. Maybe not having Jason around this summer and getting this writer's book is a sign. I'll have plenty of free time. . . .

Maybe it's time for me to start making my dreams happen.

2

ALMOST HAWAII

I fix dinner before Dad gets home and take it into my room. Tossing my book bag up to the top bunk, which is my brother's old bed, I sit down at the desk with my bowl of ravioli. Then I remove piles of handwritten paper and computer printouts from the two drawers.

I'll pick out my best stories, type them up so they're neat, and then go to the library and get addresses of magazines to send them to. I spear some ravioli on my fork and pop them into my mouth. If I could get one of my stories printed in a famous magazine, everyone would be impressed.

Then maybe I could write a novel that gets turned into a movie. I'll take Jason, my parents, and the Ghostwriter team to see it without telling them anything. I'd love to see their faces when they notice in the credits: *Movie based on a novel by Rob Baker*!

My hands shake with excitement as I go through the pile of stories I've written. I skim over science fiction pieces, poems, and an unfinished play. I look over the fantasy stories, reading about worlds of purple people living under silver suns. I love writing about heroes who battle evil demons and scary dragons, but big-time magazines never print stories like these.

Leaning back in my chair, I stare at the pile of stories on my desk. I want to get something published that is great. Something I can show my friends and my family that will knock them over. None of my old stuff is just right. I'll have to come up with something new.

The next morning, I wake up to the sound of my father's electric razor buzzing from the bathroom across the hall. I glance at my alarm clock and remember that I do not have to get up, shower, or go to school.

I smile to myself and roll over on my stomach, feeling under my pillow for the black spiral-bound book. Today is the first morning of *my* summer job.

The heading on the second page reads:

**Good writers write what they know.
WHAT DO YOU KNOW AND WHAT WOULD YOU LIKE TO LEARN?**

I know what my room looks like. Boring! I know about being thirteen. Big deal. Maybe writing about those things is good practice, but I don't want to do practice writing. I want to write something brilliant to sell to a magazine, so I ignore the question. I think and write, on my bed . . . at my desk . . . and at the kitchen table with a bowl of cereal. Coming up with something brilliant isn't easy.

Pages of cross-outs later, the phone rings. I get up from the table to answer it.

"Hello?" I grumble.

"Yo," Jamal says cheerfully. "Did you just fall out of bed?"

"No."

"You wanna hang with me and the team? Everybody except Tina is over at my place. She's at the dentist."

"What are you guys doing?"

"Well," Jamal says, "my sister Danitra just got a job at the new Y on Lafayette Avenue. They've got a pool."

"A cold pool?" I tug my shirt away from my sticky skin. "I could get into that." It must be ninety degrees already.

I glance at the open notebook on the kitchen table. Later. I'll work on it later.

The Lafayette Y is a gray cement building that takes up almost one whole block. It's so new, there's hardly any graffiti on the walls. Wooden benches and trash cans line the outside between two front entrances.

The five of us walk into the cavernous main hall, which has a row of video games to the right and a snack bar with little blue tables to the left.

"There's the line." Lenni points to a group of people, mostly kids, waiting behind a rope that leads past the video games, around a corner. A sign nearby reads: TO POOL. A tall security guard with a walkie-talkie dangling from his belt nods to us as we get on line.

"Do you need a towel or pool mat with your locker rental?" the teenage girl behind the counter asks.

"No," I say.

"Then that'll be one dollar to swim and one dollar to rent a locker, fifty cents of which is refunded when you return your key over there." We look where she is pointing and see Danitra behind the RETURN & REFUND sign, counting change into a woman's hand.

"Hi, little brother and friends," Danitra says as we walk past her counter.

"Nice uniform," Jamal teases.

"Please! Pink is not my style! But I get to swim and eat here for free. And I have my independence."

Two men come out of the locker room and get on line behind us to return plastic pool cushions. Danitra stands taller and waves us on. Lenni grabs Gaby's arm and pulls her toward the women's locker room.

"Meet you by the pool," she calls.

Alex, Jamal, and I change out of our jeans and T-shirts and jam everything into small metal lockers. Then we snap the elastic-banded locker keys around our wrists, rinse under the showers, and head to the pool with our towels.

"Whoa!" Alex says as we walk through the door into a cement-walled courtyard.

Sunlight bounces off the brilliant blue water of an Olympic-size swimming pool and I'm glad I came.

"Cool," Jamal says.

"Alex, over here," Gaby calls.

She and Lenni have spread their towels out near a round wading pool where little kids are splashing and sailing rubber boats.

Alex, Jamal, Lenni, Gaby . . . my friends. The team. I try these words out silently. They still feel a little weird to me.

I like these guys, but I'm just starting to know them, and they don't really know me yet. No one does, except maybe my brother. Still, it's a hot summer day. The kind of day you want to have friends.

Lenni scrambles to her feet and heads for the deep end of the pool. She leans forward and dives in from the side, headfirst.

The rest of us follow her to the side and look down into the shimmering water until she surfaces, spouting water like a dolphin.

"Come on in. It's great!"

I take a deep breath and jump in, feetfirst. The water prickles my skin; it's much colder than the ocean in Hawaii, where I lived for a while.

"Race you!" Lenni says. "To the shallow end and back."

I dive under and do the crawl across the pool with my eyes open, avoiding other swimmers. The shallow end is too crowded to do a flip, so I just turn around and head back. When I get to the other side, Lenni is there, waiting.

"You're fast," I say, surprised. I've always beaten my older brother when we race.

She smiles. "Thank you."

I shake wet hair out of my eyes. We tread water and look around for the others. They're at the opposite end of the pool. Jamal and Alex are standing in water up to their waists; Gaby is sitting on the side, dangling her feet in.

Lenni and I swim over.

"What are you guys doing over here?" I ask.

"Watch," Alex says. "I can do a handstand." He sticks his arms out and goes under. His legs rise out of the water and flail for a second, before toppling over backward. Alex comes up sputtering.

A beach ball splats on the water in front of Lenni. "It's less crowded in the deep end," she says, pushing the ball away.

"We like it here," Jamal says.

"Jamal can't swim," Gaby volunteers from the side. "Neither can I. Alex promised he'd teach me, but he won't do it today because Tina's not here to see him."

"Gaby, you have such a big mouth." Alex scowls.

"Really? You can't swim?" Lenni asks.

"Yeah, so?" Jamal says.

"It's no big deal," Lenni says quickly. "I learned one summer when I was visiting my grandma. Maybe I could teach you."

"Who says I want to learn?" Jamal moves away and starts to play catch with a group of kids.

"You can teach me to swim," Gaby says. "Is it hard?" She lowers herself into the water.

I flip onto my back and head away, circling my arms like a

windmill. The water around me feels smooth and the sky above is very blue, almost like in Hawaii.

I liked living there. Jason and I went to the beach almost every day to swim and build sand castles with stone moats and secret escape tunnels. That was before he started going away to a special school for deaf kids. I was seven when he left. I wanted to be deaf, too, so I could go with him.

Something in my throat clenches up. I stop swimming and float, studying the sky. Jason went away, but he came back every summer, until this one. This summer he ditched me to hang out with new friends from school.

I turn away from the sky and start swimming, churning my arms through the water and kicking ferociously. Back and forth, one lap, two, three . . . My eyes sting from the chlorine. How could he? He knows we just moved here and I'm starting over, again.

Our family's always moving. My mother, Jason, and I hate it, but my father likes new places. Now that he's retired from the Air Force, he promises we'll stay put for a while. He's got an office job with the Department of Veterans Affairs, which means he shouldn't get transferred as much. We'll see. I'll believe it if we're still living in Brooklyn next year.

My arms and legs burn but I keep swimming. Ten laps . . . eleven . . . I don't care. I don't care that Jason isn't coming home. I don't care if our family moves somewhere else. I don't care about anything.

When I can barely make it to the edge of the pool, I hoist myself out. Gaby is sitting alone reading a comic book. I drop onto my striped towel.

"Alex and Jamal went to play video games and Lenni's talking to one of the lifeguards," Gaby informs me.

I close my eyes. Warm sun soaks into my chilled skin. The poolside cement is hard under my towel. Half an idea for a story flits through my brain: a hobo traveling to all the places I've lived, tropical Hawaii . . . dusty, hot Texas . . . suburban New Jersey with its highways and malls . . .

"I played Scrabble with Ghostwriter yesterday," Gaby tells me. "We had fun, except it's hard for him not to cheat and read my letters."

"Did you win?" I open my eyes, shading them with one arm.

"Uh-huh. I think he let me. So, what have you been doing?" Gaby asks.

"Writing."

"When you become a famous writer, Tina and I can do a documentary about your life. We're going to be famous filmmakers, you know."

"I don't care about being famous," I say. But the minute I say it, I know it isn't true. For a second I get worried. Writers aren't supposed to care about things like fame.

"Well, who's going to buy your stuff if no one knows who you are?" Gaby asks.

She's right, I think. It's fine to be famous. Famous is okay. *If* I can actually write anything someone will want to publish.

"Do you have a pen name?" Gaby asks.

"No," I say.

Then it hits me. Of course. I need to have a memorable name, like Edgar Allan Poe or W.E.B. Du Bois. Famous writers don't have bland names like mine.

I sit up abruptly. I still feel antsy, charged-up, but I'm beginning to like it that way. It's just part of becoming a real writer.

3

DIAMONDS

In the locker room, I think about pen names while I throw on my street clothes. Langston Hughes, now that has an important sound . . . Piers Anthony . . .

Trouble is, every name that pops into my head belongs to a writer already. I need one of my own.

Heading for the door, I catch a reflection of myself in the wall-length mirror and stop short. My eyes travel past dark eyebrows to my loose white T-shirt and favorite jeans, down to the scuffed red-and-white basketball hightops on my feet. I frown at myself.

In my picture collection of talented writers, all the men have full beards, or sleek hair, or wear fancy black suits with black shirts. Not one is a thirteen-year-old kid wearing dirty sneakers and old jeans with holes in the knees. I bet the big magazines don't buy many stories from writers like me. But they might buy something from a talented writer with a fresh pen name who just happens to be thirteen. . . . It could happen. If I do it right. And I'm beginning to form a plan.

Jamal is in the main hall, playing Space War. I go over and watch him crash his last shuttle.

"High score again." He grins, entering his initials. "You want to play?"

"Nah. I think I'll head out."

"Yeah, me too," Jamal says. He nods toward the snack bar. "I already told Alex this was my last game."

We walk out of the Y into the sticky afternoon.

"Where you heading?" Jamal asks, jamming his hands into his jeans pockets.

"I have to get some stuff," I say vaguely, not sure if I want him coming with me.

We walk toward busy Fulton Street.

Jamal scuffs his sneakers against cracks in the sidewalk. "So, you think it's geeky that I can't swim?" he asks.

"No. The only reason I know how is 'cause I lived in Hawaii. Everybody knows how to swim there."

"Yeah, well maybe now that there's a pool around here, I'll figure it out." He kicks a chunk of broken sidewalk. "I hate not knowing how to do things."

"I do, too," I say, remembering each story I started this morning and then crossed out.

We turn onto Fulton and amble past burger joints, drugstores, and windows full of shoes.

"Let's go in here." I pull open the glass doors to a department store.

We stroll up and down the aisles.

"Check this out!" Jamal laughs, taking a stiff orange wig off its stand and placing it on his head. "I am your leader," he says in a mechanical Martian voice.

I roll my eyes. "You are one weird dude, Jamal." I am glad he came with me. I don't want to jinx my summer plans by letting too many people in on them, but it's nice hanging out with him.

Jamal puts the wig back and follows me to the next aisle.

"If you told me what kind of thing you were looking for, I could help you find it," he suggests.

I stop by the jewelry counter in front of the sign, EAR PIERC-ING SPECIAL: $10 WITH POST.

I look over the selection of earring studs behind the glass case. A diamond stud glints, catching my eye.

"Diamond Jones," I whisper. It's the perfect name.

"Huh?" Jamal says, leaning against the case.

I am picturing myself dressed in black with my hair slicked back and a small diamond earring in one ear. Tall and lean like a forties gangster. Or a nineties writer. A fan comes up to me, touches my arm, and says, "Aren't you the famous Diamond Jones? I loved your book!"

Jamal breaks into my daydream. "You're going to get your ears pierced?" he asks in disbelief.

"Just one," I say. "With that." I point to the diamond stud. "Isn't that the greatest writer's earring you've ever seen? Excuse me . . . " I call the saleswoman over.

"That tray is not part of the special," the saleswoman says. "Do you want the special?"

I nod. I have two five-dollar bills and seven singles in my wallet, plus a lot of change in my pocket, allowance I've saved. It has to last until July.

The woman points to a revolving case on the counter. "Then these are what you want to look at."

"Any diamonds?" I ask, slowly twirling the case.

The lady snorts. "Are you kidding?"

Nothing sparkles. "How about fake diamonds?" I ask.

"For ten bucks, you're lucky to get gold plate."

"Man, you really want to pierce your ear?" Jamal asks. "My sister got hers pierced and she said it hurt. And you gotta keep messing with them or they get infected. . . . Don't you think your parents will flip?"

"I guess," I say, looking at the diamond stud again. It is perfect, but I can't afford it and Jamal's right. My dad would hit the roof if I came home with a pierced ear. He is not very hip.

"What's this all about?" Jamal asks as we head through the audio aisle.

I look at him. I do want to tell someone.

"I'm starting my career as a professional writer," I say, lowering my voice. "Jamal Jenkins." I stick out my hand. "Meet Diamond Jones."

Jamal shakes hands with me, looking baffled.

"That's my new pen name," I explain. "All professional writers have one." I'm not sure if that's true, but it sounds good. "Now I need the right look for a writer. I have to get some stuff that will make me seem older, and artistic."

"Okay," Jamal says, getting into it. "I'll help you look. You want stuff that'll make you seem offbeat and different, right?"

"Yeah."

We split up. I check out aisles full of bedroom slippers, deodorant, and sunglasses. I find a pair of cool black shades and look for Jamal to get his opinion.

Jamal is at the end of the accessories aisle, talking to a red-headed clerk. He seems mad.

"I'm just looking, is that a crime?" Jamal says, holding out both hands.

"Calm down," the clerk says smoothly. "I just wanted to see if I could help you find anything." He turns and sees me standing there, holding the sunglasses.

"I want to show you these," I say to Jamal, unsure of what's going on.

The clerk steps away from us and starts rearranging a display of bow ties nearby.

"Look, he's going to hang there and make sure I don't steal anything," Jamal mutters. "I am so tired of this."

"What's up?"

"Nothing." Jamal shakes his head. "I found something for you," he says, selecting a thin tie off the rack. Its design of black quill pens and tiny ink bottles almost jumps off the shiny white material.

"Total Diamond Jones!" I say, reaching for it. "What do you think of these sunglasses?"

"Funky," Jamal says, hardly looking at them. He is staring at the clerk, who is watching us out of the corner of one eye.

"Let's go." I tug on Jamal's arm.

We head to the next aisle. "What is going on?" I ask.

"It's not fair," Jamal says quietly. "This kind of bogus stuff happens to me all the time! Last weekend, I went to Queens with this guy, Darryl, from school. We visited his cousin and we were all hanging out, just joking around. Then this white lady comes out of her house and starts yelling at us, 'Get out of here or I'm going to call the cops!' "

"Whoa," I say, surprised. We walk down the row of hats.

Jamal frowns. "We weren't doing anything. But she kept saying, 'We don't want any trouble around here.' Darryl figured she thought we were going to mess with her house or her car or something. Three black guys in a white neighborhood, you know?"

I stop walking. "That's stupid."

"Yeah." Jamal nods, fingering a striped red, white, and blue baseball cap. Then he shrugs. "Let's talk about something else, okay? What else does a professional writer need?"

Back home, I climb up the bunk-bed ladder and hunt through the pile of clothing on Jason's bed. Since my brother's hardly around, his bed is my second closet. I find and change into a plain black T-shirt and my black dress pants. Then I tear open the bag with the things Jamal and I picked out.

I knot the thin, shiny writer's tie around my neck. Then I unscrew the cap off the jar of hair grease and slick back my hair. In the bathroom, I check myself out. Diamond Jones looks back at me from the medicine cabinet mirror. He could use a diamond stud, but even without one, he's sleek, tough, pensive. Yes.

"Rob, dinner," my mother calls from the living room.

I saunter out to the dining table.

"It should be like this every night," my father is saying as Mom places flowered blue dishes onto straw place mats. "Families should have their dinner together, same time, every night."

"Gordon, you know the gallery is not a nine-to-five job. We have openings, receptions. . . . " She lifts the lid from a dish of corn and steam rises.

Dad glances at me as I sit down and does a double take. "What's with you?" he asks.

"Nice evening, isn't it?" Diamond Jones says, suavely spreading a napkin across his lap.

My mother looks at me and smiles. "What an interesting tie, Rob."

"Interesting? That's not the word I'd choose," Dad says. "And why are you wearing your good pants?"

"I'll have a bit of baked chicken and some mashed potatoes, please," Diamond Jones says politely, holding his plate out.

"Please change into your regular clothes," Dad says. "And wash that goop out of your hair."

Diamond Jones slowly turns his head to look at him, eye to eye. "I'm very comfortable, thank you," he says.

Dad raises his eyebrows. "You look like a punk. Go change," he says firmly.

I get up slowly from the table and go to my room. Inside, I lean against the closed door. I don't look like a punk, and anyway, my father shouldn't care if I did! I'm not hurting anybody.

I wish my dad and I got along better, but we never have. Things always have to be the way *he* wants them. Well, he can make me move all over the country and he can send my best friend away, but there's one thing he can't take away from me. I'm a writer, a real writer, and nothing he says will change that!

I sit down at my desk and remove *Writer's Truths* from the top drawer, opening it to the next clean page.

Writers write to find out what they are thinking.

WHAT IS IMPORTANT TO YOU?

Quick as a flash, a glow darts across the words. Ghostwriter is reading with me. I smile to myself. I can always depend on him to be around. Picking up a ballpoint pen, I begin to write.

4

EVERY DAY IS SATURDAY

For the rest of the week, I work in my room, as Diamond Jones. Between writing stories, I eat breakfast, lunch, and dinner in front of the living room TV. Between the TV characters, my characters, and Ghostwriter, I have lots of good company.

Early Saturday morning, I pull on a fresh black shirt with black jeans and ease into the kitchen.

"Jamal?" I whisper into the phone. I don't want to wake my parents.

"Hey, man. What's up?"

"What are you doing today?" I ask.

"Lenni and I are going to the street fair by the park. You want to come?"

"Yeah. I'll meet you on my front steps," I tell him, and hang up.

Lenni and Jamal arrive minutes later, wearing shorts and big smiles.

"Hi, Rob. Don't you love summer?" Lenni laughs. "Every day is Saturday!" She eyes my clothes. "Aren't you hot dressed like that?"

"No," I say, tugging my tie straight. I love being Diamond Jones.

The four streets surrounding Fort Greene Park are closed to traffic. Tons of people mill around, checking out booths of food, games, and free information.

"Cotton candy!" Lenni cries, rushing over to buy a large pink-and-blue puff.

We stroll the streets, stopping at every booth. I pick up pamphlets about vitamins, adoption, pet care, cable TV, and family therapy. You never know what information will come in handy for a story.

"Yo, Jamal."

Two guys wearing biker shorts and colorful nylon jackets spot us through the crowd and come over. One guy's dreadlocks are pulled back into a short ponytail. I recognize them both from school.

"Hey, Darryl. Hey, Manny," Jamal says, smiling. "What's up?"

"Not much." Darryl looks over at Lenni and me, and frowns. "What's up with you?"

"Just hanging," Jamal says. "We're thinking about getting some hot dogs. You guys want to come?"

"Nah. We're heading to the center to shoot pool," Darryl says.

Manny takes a pack of gum out of his jacket pocket. "Ms. Lewis is giving us free games if we help her move some boxes," he says, popping two sticks of gum into his mouth. "Why don't you come with us?"

Jamal smiles uncertainly. "I'm hanging out with these guys . . ."

An odd look crosses Darryl's face.

"Well, see you around." Manny waves. "Let's go, Darryl. I'm itchin' to rack up."

Darryl looks at Jamal for a second. "You know," he says, just before he turns away. "Brothers should stick together."

The three of us watch Darryl and Manny take off.

"Rude," Lenni complains. "They acted like we weren't even here."

Jamal stares into the crowd where his friends have disappeared. "I know that one," he says under his breath.

"What?" I ask.

"Never mind." Jamal's face tightens. "I'm going to get a hot dog." He strides off.

I scratch my cheek with a fistful of pamphlets. "I wouldn't have minded playing some pool."

"We weren't invited," Lenni reminds me.

"I know."

"That cotton candy made me hungry," Lenni says. "You want to check out the food booths?"

Lenni and I spot Jamal on a long line for the hot dog vendor. We get on a shorter line for pizza.

"Jamal!" Lenni yells to get his attention. "We're over here."

Jamal looks over quickly, nods, and then looks away.

Lenni and I get our food and walk back to the park fence.

We eat quietly, watching as Jamal gets his food and, instead of coming over, sits down at the curb by himself.

"What is with him?" Lenni mutters. "He's acting like *we're* the ones who were rude."

I don't know what to say, so I don't answer.

"Are you glad you moved here?" Lenni asks finally.

I shrug. "It's okay. Just another new place."

"I bet all the places you've lived and all the people you've met will give you lots of ideas for stories when you're a writer."

"I'm already a writer."

"You know what I mean," Lenni says. "I'm already a songwriter, too, but no one gets to hear my songs except me. That's going to change someday. I've been listening to my dad's band record and I'm learning new stuff all the time."

"Do you ever have a problem trying to think of something

great to write a song about?" I ask, wiping pizza sauce off my upper lip.

"No." Lenni laughs. "Practically everything makes me think of a song . . . school, my family . . . I just have trouble figuring out notes and writing the whole thing down. That's why I carry my songbook with me everywhere." She crumples up her empty paper plate and takes a sip of root beer.

I watch Jamal get up from the curb, toss his garbage in a wire trash can, and head over to us.

"Uh . . . I'm going to the community center for a while," he says. "I'll catch you guys later."

Lenni pretends like she doesn't care. "Maybe we'll go there, too."

Jamal stares at her for a long second. Then he shrugs. "Do whatever you want."

We watch him disappear into the crowd. There's a funny feeling in the pit of my stomach.

"I think I'll write a song about someone who's ditching his old friends," Lenni says quietly.

That night I come up with a great first line: *Friendship travels a two-lane highway, following, leading, and traveling side by side.* I am truly impressed with myself.

Except I used "travel" twice. I reach for my thesaurus and look it up. Crossing out the word "traveling," I replace it with "cruising." *Friendship travels a two-lane highway, following, leading, and cruising side by side.* Much better.

It's the first sentence of a magnificent short story. But . . . *What do I know about friendship?* I write. *Except for my brother, I have no real friends.*

On the page, a few letters from what I've written start to glow and rearrange themselves.

I'M YOUR FRIEND.

Hi, Ghostwriter! I write. *Thanks—but you're different.*

Ghostwriter swirls some more letters to write back, FRIENDS ARE IMPORTANT.

I've never lived in one place long enough to keep any, I explain. *Sometimes I try to stay in touch with people after my family moves, but I get one letter, maybe two, and that's it. Then I never hear from them again. It's not worth it.*

AREN'T YOU STAYING HERE?

Who knows? That's what my dad says. I'm not counting on it. I've done that before.

WHAT ABOUT THE TEAM? THEY THINK YOU'RE A FRIEND.

I chew on the end of my pen. *I know,* I write slowly. *But I don't know how to be one.*

YOU COULD LEARN.

Maybe . . . I look down at Ghostwriter's words doubtfully. *But maybe it's better for me to just depend on myself. If my family moves, are you going to come with us?*

I CAN GO ANYWHERE. YOU WON'T BE RID OF ME.

I smile and scribble, *That's good news.*

GIVE YOUR OTHER NEW FRIENDS A CHANCE,

TOO. THEY CAN AT LEAST BE FRIENDS FOR NOW, IF NOT FOREVER.

I don't believe in forever, GW, I write.

For a moment, nothing happens. Then just a few letters swirl together.

I DO.

5

HAPPY FAMILY

The next morning there's a knock on my door. I peek at the clock. 10:05 A.M. I groan and roll over in bed.

"Rob, it's Mom. Can I come in?"

She opens the door without waiting for an answer and sits down on the side of my bed in her robe. "Hi, honey. It feels like I haven't seen you in days." She rumples my hair.

"What is it, Mom?" I yank the pillow over my head.

"I've made Sunday brunch. French toast."

"Is Dad home?"

"Of course."

"I'm not hungry."

"Rob, please. You're making this extra hard on me. You know how Dad worries about this family falling apart now that I'm working again."

I push away the pillow and lean up to look at her. "I'm

making this hard? Dad's the one who's bugging you! I'm glad you're working. If the family's falling apart, it's his fault! He sent Jason away. He's the one who's always—"

Mom gives me one of her soft looks. "Rob, please . . . I miss Jason, too. But he'll be back soon enough."

I fall back on my bed. "Okay, I'll come to breakfast, but I hope Dad leaves me alone."

"You know he means well." Mom sighs. "Gruffness is just his way. Underneath he has a good heart. He wants our family to be happy, just like I do."

I roll my eyes. "He wants robots that'll do whatever he tells them."

Mom sighs again. We've had this conversation a million times.

"Come eat," she says.

Dad is sitting at the kitchen table reading the Sunday *Times*. He lowers the paper when I sit down.

"Morning, Rob," he says.

"Morning," I mumble.

Dad snaps the paper closed and puts it to the side. "How's your summer going?" he asks, trying to be friendly.

"Fine," I say, feeling uncomfortable. It's funny. When my father makes an effort to be nice, I don't know how to act.

"Remind me to give you money for a haircut," Dad says as Mom brings a plate of French toast to the table.

I stare down at the butter dish, thinking, Diamond Jones does not want a crew cut, thank you. I manage to keep my mouth shut. I don't want to start another fight.

Mom takes the jug of maple syrup out of the fridge. Cinnamon fills the air. I grab my fork and reach for a slice.

Dad clears his throat. "So, what have you been up to?"

"Not much," I say, stuffing my mouth.

"Oh, come on," Dad says. "Your mother and I haven't seen your face all week."

I put down my fork, my stomach clenching up. Why did I listen to my mother? I should have stayed in my room.

"Gordon," Mom says. "We're together now; let's enjoy it."

"I'd just like to know how my son is spending his free time," Dad complains. "Is that too much to ask?"

I look over at Mom. "You see what I mean? This never changes."

I push my chair away from the table.

"Sit down, Rob," Dad says as I stand up.

"No, thank you."

"Gordon . . . Rob . . . " Mom tries to calm us.

"Your manners are out of hand," Dad snaps. He raises his voice as I leave the kitchen. "Robert Baker!"

I don't turn back.

As soon as I am out of sight, I run into my room and throw on jeans and a T-shirt. Jamming my writer's book under the mattress of Jason's bed, I grab my sneakers and fly out of the apartment before anyone can stop me.

Heart pounding, I sit down on the front steps, slip my bare feet into hightops, and lace them up. I've never done anything like this!

I walk quickly through the warm morning air to clear my head. The Fernandez grocery store is a few blocks away. As the glistening stacks of fruit come into view, my racing heart slows down a little. I'll see if any of my friends are around. I just feel like hanging with someone right now.

The bells over the door jingle as I enter. Behind the counter, Alex looks up from a detective novel.

"Hi." He grins. "You need something?"

"Nah. I'm just—I was just passing by." I touch the yellowed edge of a Spanish cartoon taped to the back of the cash register. "You working all day or you want to go do something?"

Alex grimaces. "I'd rather hang out, but I'm in charge of the bodega till my father gets back." His face brightens. "Later he's going to show me how the books work. I'm good with money."

It must be nice to like your dad, I think wistfully. And have him teach you things. Sometimes I wish my father and I could start over.

"I guess I'll run up and see if Lenni is home," I say.

Lenni and her dad live in a big loft apartment upstairs from the bodega. When I knock on the door, she opens it.

"Hi! You're just in time to hear the new song I'm working on." She pulls me into the large loft. "How's it going?"

"Not great," I admit, flopping down onto the couch.

"What's up?" she asks.

"I just ran out on my folks in the middle of breakfast."

"How come?"

"I'm not even sure." I lean forward and rest my elbows on my knees. "My dad and I don't fight *about* anything. He just says little things that rub me the wrong way. Then I talk back, and that rubs him the wrong way. . . ."

"Does he yell at you?" Lenni asks.

"Not really. He's just used to bossing people around, so he starts treating me like I'm in the army. I hate being pushed! Your dad isn't like that, is he?"

"No." Lenni rocks back on her heels, thinking. "He's pretty laid-back. Sometimes he gets very quiet and I can't talk to him . . . but mostly we get along."

"You're lucky," I say, leaning back against the couch.

Lenni's eyes cloud up for a moment. "We're all we've got," she says.

"Sorry," I say quickly. I forgot.

Lenni shakes her head. "No. I am lucky. I love my family. It's just very small since my mom died." She smiles sadly and shrugs.

The phone rings. Lenni goes to answer it.

"Hello . . . Jamal?" She listens for a moment. "The whole

team? Well, Rob's here. I can ask him . . . I guess that sounds okay . . . See you later." She hangs up, looking puzzled.

"Danitra is cooking a big dinner and Jamal wants the whole team to come," she says. "He said Danitra learned all these African recipes at college and she wants to try them out. I don't get it. Yesterday he blew us off, and today he's acting like nothing's wrong. Are you going to go?"

"Sure," I say. At least at the Jenkinses' I'll get something to eat. Besides . . . besides, I just plain like hanging with the team. I think about what Ghostwriter said to me last night. "GIVE YOUR OTHER NEW FRIENDS A CHANCE."

Maybe he's right. Maybe it's up to me.

"Come on, Lenni, it'll be fun," I tell her.

"I guess so." She turns her electric keyboard on. "It just feels weird not knowing what's up with Jamal. Okay . . . so here's my new song." She clears her throat. "It's about blue whales."

6

THE WORLD IS WAITING

When I get to Jamal's house later that evening, the rest of the team is already sitting at the dining room table with Jamal's mom, dad, and grandma. Danitra comes out of the kitchen, dressed in a red, orange, and yellow smock, carrying a large bowl of something.

"Perfect timing," she tells me as I sit down. "Everybody, help yourself to my version of South African cuisine. This is papaya and chili soup." She sets down the large bowl. "There's chicken and groundnut stew." She points. "Be careful. It's spicy. You can tame it with the millet." Danitra touches a dish of steaming grain.

My stomach rumbles in anticipation. I love spicy food.

"The rusks are really good dipped into a sauce." Danitra points to a basket of hard, round biscuits. "There's salad . . . and warm milk tarts for dessert, so leave room." She nods at the table, pleased with herself.

"Everything looks gorgeous!" Mrs. Jenkins says, filling her plate. "What an exotic meal."

"Exotic?" Danitra frowns, sitting down. "This is food from our land."

Mrs. Jenkins smiles. "We've never been to Africa, honey," she says. "It's wonderful that you take pride in your heritage, but this whole family was born right here in America. This is our land."

Danitra taps her fork against her plate. "I don't believe you just said that. Have you forgotten that there was a time when black people were actually slaves in this country?"

Does every family do this fight scene? I help myself to stew, glad at least here no one expects me to talk.

Mr. Jenkins clears his throat. "Let's not get political," he says soothingly. "Everything is delicious, Danitra."

"Oh, a little politics is good for the digestion." Grandma CeCe smiles, pouring herself a glass of water.

"I believe that black people need to take care of each other," Danitra says to her mother. "If we don't, who will?"

Mrs. Jenkins shakes her head. "People are people. Good and bad. It has nothing to do with color. Think how you're making Jamal's friends feel," she adds sternly.

I look down, embarrassed. I don't feel bad about what Danitra is saying, especially after seeing how that dumb clerk treated Jamal in the store. It makes a lot of sense to me that he'd want to hang with his black friends sometimes. I just wish he would talk about it a little more or something.

I put some millet on my plate, then pass the bowl to Lenni. Across the table, Danitra catches my eye and gives me a big smile. I smile back.

After dinner, Danitra and Grandma CeCe clear the table, Jamal's parents go upstairs, and the rest of us head into the living room. Lenni rented this old black-and-white *Dracula* movie and we're going to watch it on the VCR.

As she pops the cassette into the VCR, Lenni looks at Jamal. I can tell that she's been thinking about the dinner conversation, too. "About what Danitra was saying," she begins, "that's why you ditched me and Rob yesterday, right? You wanted to hang out with your black friends?"

Tina, Alex, and Gaby turn to look at Jamal, surprised.

He sinks back against the couch. "Hey, you guys aren't my *only* friends," he says.

Tina hugs her knees. "You wouldn't stop hanging out with us just because we're not black, would you?"

Jamal shakes his head. "Of course not."

"Good," Tina says. " 'Cause I wouldn't stop hanging out with you just because you're not Vietnamese."

"But I want to hang out with other people, too, like Darryl

and Manny. They understand some things. . . . " Jamal's voice trails off.

I want to say, Jamal, how do you know we won't understand something if you don't tell us what it is? I want to say, Lenni, chill, it's not that big a deal if Jamal wanted to do something else yesterday. But the words don't come out. Maybe I shouldn't get involved.

"Your other friends could hang out with us," Lenni tells Jamal. "At least sometimes."

Jamal shakes his head without saying anything.

"I think people can have more than one group of friends," Alex agrees. "I like hanging with you guys, but I also like being with Latino people." He grins. "Sometimes I just wish that everyone in the world could speak Spanish. It would be so much easier."

The rest of us laugh, but Lenni is still angry. "You can't just blow off old friends for new ones," she says. "That's not fair! We had plans." She looks pointedly at Jamal.

Jamal nods, staring down at his sneakers. "I know. I'm sorry about that," he says.

I can tell he feels bad. Usually Jamal is the one who's outgoing and keeps the rest of our team together. It's weird to see him quiet and far away, the way I usually am, trying to figure things out.

After the video Tina, Gaby, Alex, Lenni, and I walk out

together. Right before we split up, Lenni reaches into her back pocket. She hands me a folded page torn from a magazine. "This is for you."

I read it under the yellow glow of a streetlight.

ANNUAL **SAVE THE WORLD** *WRITING CONTEST.*
All winners published in the Fall issue of Earth Times. *Submit short stories about ways to a happy planet Earth.*
Possible Topics: Animal rights, peace, government, race & culture, toxic waste, street violence, recycling.
Be creative and help keep our planet alive!
Deadline: July 31.
Prizes: Publication plus 1st prize = $100, 2nd = $50, 3rd = $25.
Rules: Story must be typed, double-spaced, and less than 2,000 words.

"I'd send them my whale song, but they only want short stories," Lenni says.

"This is great." I can't believe it—this contest sounds perfect for a Diamond Jones story. "Thanks, Lenni!" I say.

She grins. "Don't forget about me when everyone's asking for your autograph."

I sock her lightly on the arm and then we each head home alone.

As I walk toward my apartment I start imagining what it would be like to win the Save the World contest. I'd get published and my friends would be impressed. I wouldn't mind winning a hundred dollars either. With that kind of money I could buy a new board . . . or get my ear pierced . . . or even go visit Jason when he's back at school in the fall! I wonder if my mom and dad would let me do that.

Eating dinner with Jamal's family tonight was definitely interesting. It was weird when they were arguing, but at least now I know more about what's going on with Jamal. And it's nice to know that other families argue—not just mine!

Something scuttles across the sidewalk in front of me and I jump. A large gray rat stops and shoots me an ugly look. Heart pounding, I stamp my sneakers loudly. What if it has rabies or the bubonic plague? One bite and I could be a goner!

"Get out of here!" I yell to chase it away.

The rat ambles behind some trash cans. Then I spot another, smaller one. It darts out from under a parked car.

There were rats in *Dracula*, I remember, gray and squeaking. Ugh! I run the rest of the way home.

The apartment is dark and quiet. My parents are out. I turn on all the lights and go to my room. I am definitely weirded out.

As soon as I'm in my room, I pull out the notebook from under Jason's mattress. Right now I feel like I could write a really amazing story. But what do I write? According to the

contest rules, the story has to be about making the world a better place.

I look at my window. A dark square. Outside, the night city. The rats . . . rats. They'd be great in my story. For atmosphere. Something that Alex said at Jamal's house sticks in my mind: "I wish everyone in the world could speak Spanish."

That's an idea. If everyone in the world spoke Spanish . . . would we have world peace? Wow. That's a perfect idea for the contest. Maybe it'll be even better than *Dracula*!

Count Dracula . . . hey, there's another idea. All of a sudden this is so easy. I bite the end of my pen, forming sentences in my mind.

"Buenos días," Count Alejandro says to his guests. "I'm so glad you could come." Eyes glinting, he waves his hand toward the parlor. "Won't you join me for some . . . "

I stop. What are some Spanish words for food? Tacos? Too obvious. I squint, trying to remember some of the signs in the Fernandez bodega. Right!

"Won't you join me for some huevos and ajo?"

Yeah!

7

FAIR TO FRIENDS

Monday morning, I pull on my bathing suit, a pair of shorts, and my Hawaii surfer T-shirt, grab my skateboard, and head to Jamal's house to meet the team. Lenni lets me in.

"Thanks again," I tell her. "I stayed up late last night working on a story."

"Cool," she says, grinning. "Is it good?"

I nod confidently. "Yeah. Hey, Jamal. Can I use your computer for a little while?"

Jamal looks up from the couch where he's tying his sneakers. "Sure. When?"

"Now. I'll meet you guys at the pool."

After the team leaves, I sit down at Jamal's desk and turn on his computer. Typing up my new story, I feel happy, just like I did last night before I fell asleep. I wrote this story I really like and it will get published—I'm sure of it.

What am I going to call it?

"Count Alejandro Rules the World" I type onto the screen to see how it looks. Too long. "World Peace"?

Suddenly the words on the computer screen swirl and glow.

"WORDS FOR PEACE"? Ghostwriter suggests. "PEACE-FUL PLANS"?

Those are good titles, I type. *Hi, GW.*

I LIKE YOUR STORY.

Thanks! This is going to be the first story I get published, I think.

I CAN PICTURE COUNT ALEX IN HIS CAPE. DID THE TEAM LAUGH WHEN YOU SHOWED IT TO THEM?

I haven't shown them yet. Do you think I should?

WHY NOT?

Well, they think of me as this great writer, but they haven't seen much of my stuff yet. I want to be sure this story is really good. Maybe I'll wait and show it to them after it wins the contest and gets published in Earth Times.

I DON'T THINK YOUR FRIENDS WOULD THINK LESS OF YOU IF YOU DIDN'T WIN THE CONTEST.

My brow wrinkles up as I type. *Maybe you're right, but I don't have a lot of friends and I wouldn't want these guys feeling sorry for me in case I don't have what it takes to be a real writer. I want them to be glad I'm part of the team.*

I'M SURE THEY ALREADY ARE.

Maybe, I think. But at the moment I'm just too hyped up to get into a discussion about it. I tell Ghostwriter:

I have to go now. I'll talk to you later, GW.

I type print commands into the computer and print out two copies of my story. Then I shut the computer off and stuff my things into my book bag.

My friends are sitting around a table by the YMCA snack bar.

"Yo. I thought you'd never get here," Jamal says as I sit down. "Want some fries?" He pushes the yellow plastic basket of french fries toward me.

"Did you get your story typed?" Lenni asks.

"Yeah. It was really great of you to give me that information."

"That's what friends are for," she says. "If you read about a songwriting contest, you'd tell me about it, wouldn't you?"

"Sure."

"The burgers here are great," Alex tells me. He licks his fingers, making me hungry.

"I'm going to get something," I say, getting up. I walk over to the snack bar and study the white menu board. What do I want? Grilled cheese sandwich, fruit, muffin, meat or vegiburger, ice cream shake . . . The colorful letters on the menu board swirl and switch position to say, ROB BAKER IS A GOOD WRITER AND A GREAT FRIEND.

I quickly look behind me to see if the team has noticed. "Quit it, Ghostwriter," I hiss under my breath. Then I remember Ghostwriter can't hear me.

"What'll you have?" the guy behind the counter asks.

"A chocolate chip muffin and water," I say. "Can I borrow your pen? Just for a second?"

"I need it right back," the guy says hurriedly, handing me his ballpoint.

I grab a napkin and scribble *Thanks, GW,* feeling embarrassed as I hand the pen back.

Lenni, Alex, Gaby, and Tina are getting up as I return to the table with my food.

"No way are you going to beat me," Alex says. "I bet my score is more than all of yours together!"

"We'll see," Tina says.

"I'll stay here and keep you company," Jamal tells me. "Since I could take them all on, one-handed."

"Yeah, right," Alex says. Tina and Gaby laugh.

"Zargon doubles as soon as Rob's done eating," Jamal challenges.

"Maybe," I say as the rest of the team heads off. "Video games are not really my thing."

"That's wild." Jamal shakes his head. "I love 'em. My day was made when my sister gave me her computer."

"Your computer is great." I nod, taking a big bite of muffin.

"I'm going to ask my folks for one, next time I catch them both in a good mood."

"So—did the lucky tie help with your writing?"

"Yeah." I grin, watching Jamal's friend Darryl approach our table.

"Hey," Darryl says. "What's happening?" He looks at Jamal, ignoring me. My grin fades.

"Not much." Jamal laughs. "And that's the way I like it."

"Did you hear about the party tomorrow night? POC is renting out this whole hall."

POC? I think, leaning back in my chair.

"July 9, 1868," Darryl continues. "Black people became citizens of the U.S. of A. Check it out." He nods his head toward a bulletin board on the far wall. "The party is gonna be something. Dancing. Rappers. Comedy. My whole family is going, but I'm hanging with Manny. You want to come?"

"Yeah!" Jamal says. "I gotta ask, if it's at night, but I'm sure my parents will say yes."

Darryl holds out his fist. "Cool. See you tomorrow." He and Jamal knock their fists together lightly.

Darryl takes off and Jamal turns back to the table.

"You done eating?" he asks me.

My face feels hot. I stare at him silently. I *have* to say something, I think.

"What am I, invisible?" I ask finally.

Jamal starts shredding his napkin, looking down at the table.

"Lenni was right," I say. "Your friends are cold."

Jamal shifts in his seat uncomfortably. "Don't take it personally, man. Darryl's just not into white people."

"So, you don't care if he totally disses your other friends?" I say. "Wow. That really makes me want to hang out with you." I crumple my garbage and get up.

Jamal pushes back his chair and follows me to the trash can.

"Look, I'm sorry," he says. "It's just that he doesn't know you."

I push my paper plate through the plastic door.

"Hey. You do plenty of your own stuff without the team," Jamal goes on. "I need to do some of my own stuff, too."

"Who's stopping you? I just thought we were friends, but I guess I was wrong."

"I don't want to have to choose," Jamal says slowly.

I bend down to dig in my book bag, like I'm looking for something.

"We are friends, but . . ." Jamal pauses. Then he shrugs and turns away, heading for the video games.

I stand up and watch him cross the large room. Making friends is a stupid thing to do, I tell myself. When you let people in, they just mess you up.

I walk over to the bulletin board. In the center, there is a flyer for the party Darryl was talking about. It is sponsored by a group called People of Color. I move to the other end of the bulletin board so no one will think I'm reading it. I have more important things to do than go to parties.

Ghostwriter's glow flickers across another flyer that has dark birds drawn across the top of it.

JAY NIGHTHAWK
Reads from his new book
Poet on the Mesa
YMCA Main Hall
Saturday, June 30, 7 P.M.
Book signing & questions after the reading

Hey! I reach into my book bag for a piece of paper to jot the information down. Suddenly I *do* have more important things to do.

8

CASTLES IN THE AIR

That night I dream. I am on the beach with my brother, Jason, building a huge sand castle. It is the beach near our home in Hawaii where the sand is coarse and sticks together just right to make castle towers and rooms. The sky around us is cloudless blue and ocean pounds the shore.

Jason taps my shoulder as I finish decorating one tower with pieces of shell and coral.

"Let's go in," he signs.

"In the water?" I ask.

"No, inside . . ." He lowers the driftwood drawbridge.

On hands and knees, Jason crawls around to the ditch that connects the castle's moat to the ocean. He puts one foot into the ditch and carefully moves toward the sand castle entrance. "Come on," he waves.

I crouch down and follow him, knowing we're way too big to fit through the castle door.

But suddenly I find myself crawling on cold stone tile. I squat on my heels and look around at clamshell chairs and seaweed curtains.

"I don't believe this!" I breathe.

"This is the best castle we ever built," Jason signs proudly, standing up.

"Rob! You're here!" Lenni hikes up her long purple dress and hurries over to pull me to my feet.

"What's going on?" I ask as she pushes me toward the castle's main hall.

"Everybody's waiting, Rob. Did you forget you were reading tonight?"

The main hall is huge and filled with people seated on clamshell chairs. They start to clap when I enter the room.

"I loved your piece in *Earth Times*," a lady in a feathered hat says to me.

"It's based on his Brooklyn friends," someone says. I look to the voice. It's Alex, dressed in a long black cape. "Hi, buddy." He grins.

I head for the front of the room, dazed. The crowd cheers and applauds.

"That's our son," Dad hollers. He and Mom are holding hands, up front. They smile broadly. "We always knew he was talented," I hear my father tell the person next to him.

I stand behind a wooden podium and gaze out at the happy crowd. How did I get famous without realizing it?

Birds chirp loudly. A car honks. I wake up to the early morning sounds of Dekalb Avenue outside my window. I lie in bed feeling snug and surprised, just like I did in the sand castle hall, facing all those people who wanted to hear me read. I can't wait to really *be* famous!

I climb out of bed, sit down at my desk, and remove the two printed copies of my newest story from my book bag. Rereading it, I smile. It's so good, and important. This is the piece that's going to help me get where I was in my dream.

I dig through my desk for an envelope, find one, put a stamp on it, and carefully copy the address of *Earth Times* onto the front. Then I fold up one copy of my story, "Peace Words," and seal it in the envelope.

I hurry out to the corner mailbox. As I drop the envelope through the slot, I have a brilliant idea. I'll hold a reading, just like the one I saw advertised at the Y. I can set up the living room and read my story to the team. Ghostwriter was right. Why should I wait until the story is published? I know my story is something else. I can't wait to hear everybody's reaction!

Tuesday evening, while my folks are out to dinner, I place chairs from our dining table on each side of the living room couch so there is a row of seats facing the center of the room.

Then I cut thin slices of cheddar cheese and place them on a tray with crackers, which I put on the living room coffee table. Next to the tray, I put the bottles of soda and the paper cups Mom got me this afternoon. My father's tall reading light gets moved behind the couch for a spotlight, and the stage is ready.

I go to my room and dress in Diamond Jones black, good pants, dressy black shirt, and black shoes. There is a lump of excitement in my stomach. I have to knot my writer's tie three times before I get it to hang straight. I guess I'm nervous. I've never done anything like this before.

I slick back my hair, careful not to stain my clothes. And then I'm done. The tough, intense Diamond Jones looks back at me from the bathroom mirror. Too cool.

The doorbell rings. This is it! I go to let my audience in.

The team gets comfortable, joking around, until I dim the lights and switch on Dad's reading lamp. When Diamond Jones steps into the spotlight, they grow quiet. I hold my copy of "Peace Words" out in front of me and begin to read:

"Buenos días," Count Alejandro says to his guests. "I'm so glad you could come." Eyes glinting, he waves his hand toward the parlor. "Won't you join me for some huevos and ajo?"

Alex starts to laugh. I look up.

"This is great," he says. "Go on."

Lord Jamaal's handsome dark face wrinkles into a frown. "Are the others here? If they're not coming, this is a waste of our time." The lord's two henchmen nod.

"They'll be along." Count Alejandro takes Lord Jamaal's arm and leads him into the parlor with the two bodyguards following. "Please, have a seat." The count gestures to a red velvet couch.

"Gabriela," Count Alejandro calls his sister.

A small Spanish girl scurries into the parlor, carrying a silver tray of fancy appetizers as a gong sounds through the mansion. The count strides through the long hall to the door, his cape billowing behind, and returns to the parlor with two travelers from the North and one from the Orient.

"Lord Jamaal and countrymen," the count says formally. "May I present to you Prime Minister Lennibelle, Noblewoman Tinasan, and President Diamond Jones. Eat, please," he encourages the new guests.

Count Alejandro takes a few steps back and watches his guests dine on the delicious food. A slow smile creeps over his face.

"As you know," he says, lowering himself onto a chair across from the others, "for quite some time I have wanted everyone to speak in my native tongue. Spanish is, after all, the most beautiful language in the world and the right choice for a world language. Isn't that right, Gabriela?"

By the time I get to this part, I'm really into the story. I'm reading slowly and clearly, taking on the voices of the different guests as they each refuse to make Spanish the world language. I use a really wicked voice for the count as I read the part about how he slips the guests a sleeping potion, then drags them off to a dungeon that's crawling with rats. The count cackles loudly as he reaches into his cape and removes a vial of magical powders. "Now I will hypnotize my guests into learning my native tongue," he says. And as he enchants them one by one, they wake up speaking Spanish.

At last Count Alejandro reaches the cell where President Diamond Jones is being held. Suddenly Alex snorts. I glance up. On the couch, Gaby is picking at a scab on her knee. Lenni smiles at me. Jamal rolls his eyes. Something is wrong.

I swallow, feeling a tightness in my dry throat, as I hurry on toward the end of the story.

> The famous President Diamond Jones is sitting up on his cot, rubbing his head as the sleeping potion wears off. "What are you doing?" he cries when he sees the count holding the vial of enchanted powder. Diamond Jones leaps to his feet and knocks the vial out of the count's hand. The tiny container flies across the cell, spilling a fine spray of magical dust on the stone floor where it lands.
>
> "No!" shrieks the count. He falls to his knees and tries to sweep the glittering powder together. "I have to hypnotize all of you or my plan won't work!"
>
> "What plan?" Diamond Jones asks, yanking the count to his

feet. *"I thought you were a good man!"* He spins the count around and shakes him by the front of his cape.

"I am! Cooperate with me," the count pleads. *"Teach your people to speak Spanish and we will have world peace."*

"That's not the way to do it," Diamond Jones says. He pushes the count onto the cot with disgust. *"Controlling others is not the way to world peace. Many evil men have tried. People have to agree to be peaceful!"*

"You're right," the count says sadly. *"But Spanish is such a beautiful language."*

"Yes, it is," Diamond Jones agrees. *"But so is English, and Vietnamese, and every other language. People can speak different languages and still get along. Since you've learned my language, I'd be happy to learn yours."*

"You would?" Count Alejandro asks in disbelief.

"But not if you try to force me to," Diamond Jones says firmly. *"I would learn your language because that would be fair, and also fun."*

"How reasonable you are. No wonder you are president of your country."

"Let's break the spell on the others and start talking," Diamond Jones says. *"The world is waiting."*

THE END

When I finish reading, only Lenni and Tina clap.

"If you win the contest, are you going to split the money with us?" Alex asks with narrowed eyes.

Tina jumps in. "I liked the count, but you didn't describe the other characters as much."

"Yeah," Gaby says, looking hurt. "All Gabriela did was bring in food and follow her brother around."

"While Rob was the hero," Jamal says. "That figures."

"Yeah, really," Alex agrees. "How come you made me this evil guy who brainwashes people?"

"It's Rob's story," Lenni argues, shifting in her seat to look at Alex. "He can write it any way he wants. Even if that means all I get to do in the story is faint." She's smiling as she says this, but I don't think it's funny.

"When you make a movie, you have to get permission from people you want to film," Tina says thoughtfully.

I stand in the warm spotlight, my sweaty fingers clutching the typed pages. I thought the team would love seeing themselves in my story. And I thought they'd see that it wasn't really about them—it was about world peace, about making a difference. Didn't they like anything about it?

"Somebody should have asked my permission for this," Jamal says. "I don't want anybody calling my friends 'henchmen,' in a magazine or anyplace else." He glares at me. "'Bodyguards' . . . you are so bogus, Rob. Just because you don't like my friends. Or is it just because they're black? Why don't you just call them 'hit men' or 'guys from Jamal's gang'?"

"I—I didn't mean that," I stammer.

"Well, that's what it sounded like." Jamal scowls. "You could have just called them 'friends' or 'advisors' or something."

Lenni shakes her head. "You can't tell him what to write! What about freedom of expression?" she asks.

"What about not hurting your friends?" Gaby retorts.

"Some things aren't accurate," Tina volunteers. "Like, calling my character Tinasan makes her sound Japanese, but then you say she's Vietnamese. There's a big difference—to me, anyway."

Alex leans back in his chair. "You know, I liked the language idea, but how come you said Gaby is Spanish and Jamal is black, but you don't bother to point out that you and Prime Minister Lenni are white?"

"Yeah," Jamal agrees. "Like it's the normal thing to be white, so you only point out who isn't."

Tina starts to say something else, but I raise my arms to cut her off. My face is on fire, and I feel like I can't breathe. This is awful.

"Look, forget you ever heard this story," I say, trying to keep my voice steady. "I'll write *Earth Times* a letter and tell them I don't want to be in their contest after all."

"Don't do that," Lenni says angrily. "It's a good story. It just needs a little work. I would hate it if my friends told me

I shouldn't sing a song I wrote just because they didn't like what it said!" She glares at the others.

"Well, I vote for pulling it," Jamal says to me. "And don't put me in any more of your stories. My life is confidential."

"I believe in freedom of expression," Tina says slowly. "But I don't think people should do things that will hurt other people. There's enough of that in the world already."

Lenni looks at everyone in disbelief. "Rob didn't write *facts* about us that weren't true. He just made up a story. The whole thing is fiction. I don't think Alex is an evil count or Rob's this super-smooth guy. It's just a story!"

"That's true," Alex says, thinking it over. "I could like it better, but it is just a story, and I think censorship is bad."

"It's a tie," Jamal says stiffly. "What's your vote, Gaby? Should Rob publish his story or not?"

Gaby's eyes fill with tears. She gets to her feet. "I don't want to vote," she says quietly, leaving the room.

The rest of us sit there, stunned, as the front door shuts behind her.

Jamal shakes his head. "Way to go, Diamond Jones," he says.

Lenni shoots Jamal a look. "Why don't you let up on Rob? You know he didn't mean anything."

I run out of the apartment, spot Gaby at the end of the block, and chase after her.

"Gaby, wait! I'm sorry." I grab her arm.

"Leave me alone," she says, pulling away. "I don't want to talk to you."

"I'm sorry, Gaby. I didn't mean to hurt your feelings."

"Well, you did," she says. "And I thought you liked me."

"I do," I say, surprised.

"No, you don't." She frowns. "You think I'm just a little kid following my brother around."

"Well, you do follow Alex around a lot," I say.

"I *used* to." Gaby scowls at me. "Before I made my own friends and became part of the team. Anyway, I also tell jokes, and make videos with Tina, and do karate—better than a lot of the bigger kids in my class! How come you didn't put any of those things in your story?"

"I don't know," I say. I want to tell her again that my story didn't include those things because it's not really about her or the team, but I'm not sure of anything anymore, except how bad I feel.

She scuffs her sandals against the sidewalk.

"Look—Gaby, I'm really sorry," I say. "I didn't mean to hurt your feelings, honestly. I really . . . I like all you guys. You're my friends."

For a moment Gaby stands at the corner and doesn't budge. That's it. There's nothing I can do. I blew it and that's all. My shoulders slump and I start heading back to my place.

Then I hear her voice behind me. "I do have one suggestion."

I turn and look at her. "What?"

A small smile creeps over her face. Then she runs to catch up with me. "Get help with your Spanish. Nobody serves eggs and garlic as a fancy appetizer!"

FAME

I remember lying by the Y pool and telling Gaby that I didn't care about being famous. Even then, I knew it wasn't true. I should have seen what was happening. I got wrapped up in being the cool writer Diamond Jones and winning the contest. I couldn't wait to see my name in print. I didn't care about actually writing anymore. I just wanted everyone—especially my new friends—to think I was something special. But I blew it. Now they think I'm a creep!

For the next few days, I become a hermit. I hang out at home, alone. On Thursday, I catch myself reaching under Jason's bed for *Writer's Truths*, out of habit. But I stop myself. I don't feel like writing. Maybe I won't, ever again.

Saturday morning, I get a postcard from Jason. It depresses me even more. He's having a great time while I'm discovering that I'm a terrible writer and an awful person.

I trudge out of my room to get something to munch on and see if the TV is free. Mom and Dad are on the living room couch with a week's worth of newspapers spread out all around them.

"Hi, sweetie," Mom says. She gives me a concerned look. "Is anything wrong? You seem glum."

Dad glances up over the top of a business section.

For a second, I want to curl up on the couch between them. But I'm way too old to do that, and besides, they wouldn't understand. Mom would start babying me and Dad would probably roll his eyes and say, "You're upset about something you wrote? You'll get over it." My father doesn't take creative writing very seriously.

So I tell Mom, "I'm fine."

That night, I walk over to the Y for the reading I saw advertised. I'm so mixed up about writing that I'm not sure I even want to go anymore. But it does feel good to be out of the house.

I've never been to the Y at night. It looks different. The snack bar chairs are stacked on the blue tables and pulled into one corner. Metal folding chairs are set up in rows before a small wooden stage. About thirty adults mill around, talking to each other and reading the bulletin board. I take a seat by myself near the front.

At exactly seven o'clock, a tall man steps onto the stage,

carrying a glass of water and a book. He is wearing jeans, cow-boy boots, and a white shirt. Shiny dark hair hangs to his waist. The man leans toward the microphone.

"Good evening," he says. "I'm Jay Nighthawk. I love being a writer. I love stepping outside my home every morning to write in the shade of a scraggly tree. I love getting checks in the mail from my publisher . . . "

The audience laughs.

"And I love coming to places like this to spend time with people like yourselves." He takes a sip of water and smiles. "I do not love it when my writing hasn't sold in a while and there is no money to fix my car. In those times, I do other things besides writing in order to put gas in the tank. My job title is pretty long these days: author-carpenter-dishwasher-tour guide."

Everyone laughs again. I lean back in my seat, sadly watch-ing the man on the stage. This is so much like that dream I had; only in my dream, people wanted to listen to *me*.

The author bends over to put down his glass of water. Then he straightens up and opens the thin book.

"I try to always tell my truth," he says. "As you will see." He begins to read in a low, musical voice.

THE AMERICAN DREAM
Fans of the Atlanta Braves
pumped their arms, tomahawk chop

World Series, 1991
I watched on my new color TV

The fans were American white
in feathered headdress and painted faces
They were happy wearing sacred dress
as costume
No one meant to make fun

Stomach sour
I reached for another barbecued burger
greasy fries
Until my neighbor told me
Jay, you're not eating right
Our bodies survive the wild
At 300 pounds, you are not wild
Heavy from store-bought junk
your Indian heart will die

He was an old man
I did not want to listen
I wore my blue jeans proudly
kept my eyes on the TV
Sometimes I was able to forget
certain things about being Indian
but not really

One day the old man
took me to his home and showed me

beans, seeds, acorns from live trees
This is our food, he said
It will help you run the mesa
and talk to the sky

Young man, look, he said
sifting brown beans
between gnarled fingers
Food!

I shook my head
I did not recognize it

The room is silent when Jay Nighthawk looks up from his book. Then it bursts into applause.

I am blown away. I can picture the handful of shiny beans and feel Jay Nighthawk just wanting his old neighbor to leave him alone so he can watch TV and forget about everything. That's how I've felt all week.

After reading five more poems, the tall man closes his book. "Now I'll take some questions," he says.

"How long does it take you to write a poem?" a lady asks from the back of the room.

Jay Nighthawk laughs. "Anywhere from a day to a year. I do a lot of rewriting to make sure whatever I write is as good as it can be."

"How do you know what to change?" the lady asks.

"Oh, I sit down with a group of other writers and we hash things out. The funny thing about me is, when I first write something I always think it's wonderful. But if I sit with it for a while, I start seeing flaws. I find, the more time I take to fix a piece, the fewer rejection slips I get in the mail."

I look behind me to make sure no one I know is here. Then I raise my hand.

"Yes? Stand up, please."

I stand, my heart pounding loud in my ears. "Do you think, when someone writes a story with characters that sort of resemble real people, they should show it to those people before they send it off to get published?"

"Good question," the author says, rubbing his chin. "*Very* good question. I don't think you *have* to, but I think most real people like to see what's being written about them before it shows up in print. They can sometimes offer an author good advice. Not that a writer has to use any piece of advice he or she gets. I tend to make characters up myself, using quirks from many people. That way no one gets their feelings hurt or decides to sue me."

The man on the stage smiles at me as I sit down. To my left, a bearded man stands up.

"How long did it take you to become a writer?" he asks.

"I've always been a writer," Jay Nighthawk replies. "Ever since I was a kid, I've made up stories and scribbled them into notebooks, but I didn't get anything published until I was thirty-one years old."

Wow, I think. He's just like me. Making up stories. No matter what, I can always get lost in my stories of brave heroes in wild jungles. Brave heroes who love to travel and have life-long friends.

Mr. Nighthawk's stuff is so good, I can't believe it took him that long to get published. Maybe I shouldn't give up yet. Just because I wrote one story that stank doesn't mean I have *NO* talent.

When there are no more questions, Jay Nighthawk steps off the stage and sits at a table to sell and autograph his book. Since Mom gave me July's allowance this morning, I get on line to buy one.

"You were great," I say nervously, when it's my turn. "I learned a lot. Thanks."

"You're welcome." Jay Nighthawk reaches for a book from the neat pile beside him and asks, "Who am I signing this to?" He turns back the stiff cover.

I think about saying *Diamond Jones*, but when I open my mouth, I hear myself say, "Uh . . . Rob, Rob Baker."

"I've been thinking about your question," he says while scrawling something into my book. "Are the people in your story from a different race or culture than you?"

"Yes," I say, startled.

"Then I think it is important to show it to them and make sure you're getting certain details right." He looks up and hands me the book. "As an Indian, I'm real tired of seeing stories about Native American princesses, if you know what I mean. When I read stories like that, I know the writer didn't do any homework."

"I didn't think about that," I admit. In my head, I hear Tina say, *Calling my character Tinasan makes her sound Japanese, but then you say she's Vietnamese. There's a difference.* Boy, was I stupid.

The poet looks me in the eyes. "These are important issues. But I think the most important thing for a writer to remember is what I said before I started reading, about writing my truth. You have to write *your* truth. That's the other side of the equation. Write what's true and important to you. Satisfy yourself. If you do that, chances are you'll satisfy your readers, too."

I feel like a hundred doors are opening in my mind, but all I can say is "Wow."

Mr. Nighthawk smiles. "Good luck."

I walk away from the table and open his book, *Poet on the Mesa.* Inside is written:

> *Mr. Baker,*
> *Enjoy the road you're on. I hope to see your work someday.*
>
> > *Best,*
> > *Jay Nighthawk*

I walk home in the cool, dark air. Alone in my room, I dig under Jason's bed for my notebook. After not using it for almost a week, the black spiral-bound book feels unfamiliar in my hands. I open it to a half-filled page.

Ghostwriter? I write. *Are you there?*

HI, ROB.

Remember that story I was so into? I messed up. The team didn't like it and I wrote some dumb things.

IT'S NEVER TOO LATE TO CORRECT A MISTAKE, Ghostwriter responds.

I rest my elbow on the desk and lean my head against my left hand. *I guess so,* I scrawl gloomily. *But I feel lousy. Writing doesn't seem fun anymore.*

I used to love writing, just like Jay Nighthawk. Why did I give up the fun and get so into being famous?

Maybe because I wish I could be the brave hero with lifelong friends. Somebody with a life they don't have to escape from.

A flurry of letters rearrange themselves on the page.

I THINK WORDS CAN BE FUN AND INTERESTING. BUT THEY ARE ALSO VERY POWERFUL. YOU MUST THINK CAREFULLY ABOUT HOW TO USE THEM JUST RIGHT.

Yeah. I didn't think much at all when I first wrote the story, I write, knowing exactly what Ghostwriter means.

What if, for some reason, *Earth Times* does publish my story just the way it is. I don't want it to seem harmful, or dumb! It was supposed to be a story about making a difference! I turn to a blank page, hoping Ghostwriter is right that it's never too late to fix mistakes.

PEACE WORDS

For the next two weeks, I rework my story. I add sentences and take sentences out. I change character names and personalities. I go to the library, looking up stuff about my characters' backgrounds. I ask Tina's mother about Vietnamese words. I take breaks and slam baskets with Alex in the park. Then I go back to my desk. Writing really feels like a job. It's different, but I like it. I think.

Two Fridays later, I call Jamal to ask if I can use his computer. He is surprised to hear from me. We haven't seen each other around much lately.

"My story is done. After I type it up, I want to read it to you guys," I tell him, a familiar knot of nerves in my gut.

I've decided, if the story sounds better this time, to me and to the team, I'm going to send a copy to *Earth Times* with a letter explaining everything. But if it still doesn't work, I'll send *Earth Times* a letter asking them to drop me from their contest. Some authors don't get published until they're thirty-one; it doesn't have to happen for me right now.

Jamal opens his front door. "Long time no see," he says, not unfriendly. I follow him into his room. "You want me to get the team together for later?"

"Sure. That'd be great."

We look at each other awkwardly.

"Where's your lucky tie?" Jamal asks.

"I'm not wearing it much these days," I admit. "It's kind of hard to write all day with something around my neck."

"You were a riot that day we went shopping," Jamal tells me. "Diamond earring, hair grease . . . The famous Diamond Jones."

"Yeah." I shrug, embarrassed. "I should work on my writing first, before I work on my look, huh?"

Jamal shuffles his feet against the carpet. "How's it going?" He nods to the notebook under my arm.

"We'll see . . . " I put my notebook down on his desk.

"Okay, I can take a hint," Jamal says, turning to go. "I'm out of here."

"Later." I take a deep breath and sit down in front of the computer, turning it on.

"Ummm . . . listen," Jamal says from the doorway. His words come out in a rush. "I wanted to tell you I'm sorry things got messed up this summer. You know, hanging out with you and with my other friends. I was kind of rough on you about your story. . . . I've just got a lot on my mind."

I shake my head. "I was really dumb. My story wasn't supposed to insult anybody. I really don't think all black people belong to gangs and stuff."

"I know." Jamal nods. "And I don't think all white people are bogus. It's just hard. Everybody's got different ideas . . . I wish everybody could get along."

"Don't sweat it," I say. "I wish *I* had tons of friends wanting me to hang out with them." I look away. "I'll let Ghostwriter know when I'm done, okay?"

"Yeah." Jamal sighs from the doorway. He turns to go. "You were right about one thing, Rob. Friends shouldn't blow each other off, no matter what."

Four and a half hours later I hand Gaby seven printed pages. "Will you read it for me?" I ask.

She smiles, gets to her feet, and makes a big deal of clearing her throat.

"Ladies and gentlemen, 'Peace Words' by Mr. Robert Baker," she says. Then she begins to read.

> *"Buenos días,"* Count Alejandro says to his guests as he draws the mahogany door wide. It opens with a squeak. *"I'm so glad you could come."*
>
> Eyes sparkling, he waves a hand toward the parlor. *"Won't*

you join me for some appetizers and wine? My sister, Gabriela, has prepared her specialties for your enjoyment."

Lord Jamaal's handsome face wrinkles into a deep frown. "Are the others here? If they're not coming, this is a waste of our time." The two heads of state by Lord Jamaal's side nod silently, looking displeased. All three men wear robes of colorful African kente cloth, as is their custom.

"They'll be along." Count Alejandro takes Lord Jamaal's arm and leads the men into his parlor. "Please, have a seat." He gestures to a red velvet couch.

The count watches his three guests make themselves comfortable. This is a moment he has been waiting for for years.

"Gabriela," he calls.

A slim young woman dressed in black walks into the parlor, carrying a silver tray as a gong sounds throughout the mansion. The count strides through the long hall to the door, cape billowing out behind him, and returns to the parlor with two pale travelers from the North and one from the Orient.

"Lord Jamaal and countrymen," the count says formally. "May I present to you Prime Minister Robert, President Lennibelle, and Noblewoman Tinang. Eat, please," he encourages the new guests.

"The empanadillas are stuffed with smoked salmon," Gabriela informs everyone. "From our newly cleaned river." She kisses the tips of her fingers. "It had a good life, so it is full of flavor, like no other salmon you have tasted."

The bedroom is quiet except for Gaby's voice. I stare at the smudges of city grime on my sneakers as she reads. My story is better. I know it is. This time I've made sure that the details are accurate and that the characters are much more real and alive. I smile to myself and think, Jay Nighthawk would approve.

But as I listen to Gaby reading my words, I also wonder about the other part of what Jay Nighthawk said—about writing my own truth. With this story I've been so caught up in getting published and impressing my friends . . . I'm not sure I know what my own truth is. I decide that this is something I need to think about and work on some more. But for now, I like my story.

Finally Gaby finishes. "The end," she reads with a flourish.

"Hey, Rob," Jamal says.

I force myself to look up. Jamal grins and gives me a thumbs-up. I look around at the others. Lenni and Tina stick their thumbs out, smiling. A brilliant ball of light zings from the pages in Gaby's hand to a sports poster on the far wall. Letters on the poster switch position to glow, WAY TO GO, ROB!

"Your Spanish is on this time." Alex laughs. "With a little help from your friends."

"I like the story now," Gaby says softly. "I don't feel bad anymore."

"I still don't like being the bad guy," Alex says. Then he adds, slowly, "But you know what? The story makes sense to me now. And I think that's what's most important."

I nod, thinking of Jay Nighthawk, and knowing exactly what Alex means.

Jamal stands up. "So, what do you say, Diamond Jones? Want to hit the pool?"

I carefully fold up the story and place it in the envelope with my letter of explanation to *Earth Times*.

Jamal puts his hands on his hips. "Don't tell me you're going to go home now and work on another story."

"No way." I grin, dropping my other letter—the one asking *Earth Times* to take me out of the contest—into Jamal's recycling basket. "I need a vacation!"

The team walks me outside to the blue mailbox at the corner. I open the slot.

"Good luck," Gaby says to the envelope as it drops down. "I hope you win."

"Me, too," I say.

But really, at the moment, I don't even care. The last two weeks were hard and I'm glad they're over. Suddenly I feel light as a pigeon, as if I could just take off and circle the brownstone buildings and busy city streets. I did the best I could, and now I'm going to take a summer vacation. I can always write. Maybe I'll even be a professional writer someday. But for now I want to have some real-life fun before school starts up again.

WHAT'S NEW?

The first day of school arrives way too soon. A new locker. New teachers. But mostly the same kids. And somehow, going back to school with people I know is not all that bad. I eat lunch with Jamal, Lenni, and Alex. And after school, Alex and I shoot some baskets at the park.

When I get home that evening, my father is on the living room couch, half watching the TV news while working on a crossword puzzle.

"You got some mail," he says, nodding toward the coffee table.

An oversize picture postcard of an ornate German castle rests on top of the pile of opened bills and catalogs. Jason!

August 28 —

Hi, Squirt!
Thanks for your mail! This is my last postcard from

Germany. By the time you get it, you'll probably be back in school and so will I. I had a fantastic summer exploring small Dörfer (towns) with my buddies. We walked curved sidewalks between trim little box houses and bought sausages, bread, and custard pastries at butcher and baker shops. We'd take our food and hike uphill into sunny cow pastures to eat. Very relaxing.

It was great to be away from the big city of Washington, D.C., but I am glad to be going back. Sleeping at a different youth hostel every four days gets old. It'll be nice to be back in my regular bed with just one roommate!

Mom said you guys are staying put for another year, so expect me home for the holidays.

Love, Jase

I'm about to head off to my room when I notice, resting on top of the pile of mail, an envelope with my name and address typed on it. From *Earth Times* magazine! I snatch the envelope up and hurry to my room, ripping it open. I can't wait to show the team!

The letter inside is brief.

Dear Mr. Baker:

Thanks for your recent submission to our **SAVE THE WORLD** *contest. We regret to inform you that your entry was not selected.*

We wish you luck placing your story elsewhere.

Sincerely,

Earth Times
Editors

Underneath the typed words someone has scrawled, *Nice second try. Keep writing!* in blue pen.

I drop onto my bed. I knew that my story wasn't perfect, but this still feels so terrible. After all that worrying and re-writing and having Alex coach me in Spanish . . . after all that, I didn't win. Not even third prize?

Ghostwriter zips over the page. Individual typed letters begin to move.

SORRY, Ghostwriter glows. His glow moves up in the letter and highlights one sentence. WE WISH YOU LUCK IN PLACING YOUR STORY ELSEWHERE.

I reach into my book bag for a pen and brace the thin sheet of paper against my knees.

Elsewhere? I write. *Who else is going to want this story? It was perfect for* Earth Times—*and they didn't want it.*

Ghostwriter rearranges some letters to write, ARE YOU GIVING UP?

I flop back against my pillow, my legs dangling off the side of the bed. What am I going to tell the team? Hey, guys, remember the story I wrote this summer that we all argued about? Well, it was lousy after all. . . .

I lift my arm up and hold the letter above my head. Ghostwriter's last message is still glowing vividly.

ARE YOU GIVING UP?

I get to my feet, take the writer's book Jason sent me out of my desk drawer, and stuff the rejection letter inside. Whatever made me think I could be a writer? I'm not Mark Twain or Jay Nighthawk . . . somebody with an interesting life to write about. I'm just a boring kid who makes things up in his head to pass the time.

Mom calls me for dinner. I trudge out to the dining table, trying to push one phrase out of my mind: *Your entry was not selected.* It doesn't matter. Getting a story published isn't so important. There are a lot of other things going on in my life now. I haven't even been writing lately; I'm too busy doing things with my friends, starting eighth grade. My summer job as a writer is over.

Mom comes to the table with a casserole dish. "What's new with you two?" she asks Dad and me.

I look down at my empty plate. If only I had something good to say.

SPIKE!

The next day, after my last class, I meet up with my friends on the steps outside the school building.

"It is too hot," Jamal says. "Let's go to the Y."

"Great idea." Lenni nods. "Pretty soon we won't be able to go swimming. I hear they're shutting down the pool at the end of this month until next summer."

"I have to pick up Gaby," Alex says, tugging at his shirt collar. "Meet you there."

"I'll meet you there, too," I say thoughtfully. "There's something I have to do first."

I drop my skateboard to the ground and head to the library.

The librarian behind the reference desk hands me a fat copy of this year's *Writer's Market*. I sit down with it at a quiet table. I couldn't sleep last night, thinking about my story. I know it's good and I want to get it published. That's what writers do.

Uncapping my pen, I look through the thick book and start copying down names and addresses of magazines that publish short stories. If *Earth Times* won't print my story, maybe somebody else will.

When I get to the Y, the rest of the team is already out back by the pool. I am so hot and sweaty, I drop my towel and jump right in. My skin sizzles as I break the surface and plunge into eight feet of cold water. It feels great.

"We were wondering where you were," Lenni calls, swimming over. "Want to race?"

The pool is fairly empty. Lenni and I take off, swimming the length of the pool and back. I win.

"You held your breath the whole last stretch, didn't you?" Lenni gasps as we clutch the side of the pool.

"That's the only way I can match you!"

"My dad calls me a water baby." She grins. "One more time? How about just down to the other end. I want to see if I can hold my breath all the way across."

When we come up for air at the shallow end of the pool, Gaby pounces through the water to us.

"Look, I'm swimming," she says, flapping her arms excitedly and moving forward, one foot still touching the pool floor.

"That's good." Lenni smiles.

"Rob, check this out," Alex calls.

I look around the sunny pool. He and Tina are a few feet away, doing handstands. Alex is getting much better at keeping his legs up straight. "Look what else I can do," he says. He walks out a little deeper and does first a front somersault and then a backward one.

"Wow. Let me try that," I say, heading over. "Did you hold your nose?"

"Yes." Alex shows me. "And you tuck your head down, like this."

I try a front somersault, twist crookedly, and come up dizzy with water clogging my ears.

"It takes skill," Alex says proudly.

I start laughing. "You're right." I guess lots of things are harder than they look. But with practice, I'll get it.

I spot Jamal over by the lifeguard chair talking to his friends Darryl and Manny. Jamal seems excited about something. Manny shrugs and nods at whatever Jamal is saying. Darryl glances toward the pool.

"Look, I'm REALLY SWIMMING!" Gaby shrieks from behind me. I turn and catch a glimpse of her just before she goes under. Lenni reaches for her and Gaby comes up sputtering.

"You have to keep kicking." Lenni laughs.

"I did it for a second! Did you see me?" Gaby beams.

"Yo, guys, want to play some water volleyball?" Jamal asks, coming into the pool with his friends and wading over to us.

"We've got even teams," Manny adds, looking us over. He pats the red rubber ball under his arm.

The rest of us stare at him and Darryl. Darryl's looking at something way off in the distance.

"You want to play with us?" Lenni asks Darryl, raising one eyebrow. She crosses her arms in front of her chest. "Since when?"

Darryl glances over at Jamal. "Since now," he says with a shrug and half a smile. "Can you hang? Or is volleyball not your thing?"

"I can hit a ball." Lenni sniffs.

"So let's play!" Jamal grabs her arm. "It'll be fun. I get Lenni, Darryl, and Rob."

"Okay. We'll cream you guys, right, Alex?" Tina says, smiling at her teammates.

Manny looks at Alex. "That was a fresh somersault you did."

"Thanks," Alex says modestly.

They move away with Tina and Gaby to stand in a crooked row.

"Heads up," Darryl calls, serving.

Tina puts her wrists together and bumps the ball back across an imaginary net. Jamal jumps up and whacks it back to Alex. Alex makes two fists and hits a fast one toward me. It's just out of my reach.

I dive for the red rubber ball and knock it to Lenni as I go under. My head pops out of the water just in time to hear her yell "Spike!" as the ball splats between Alex and Manny.

"One point for our team!" Lenni grins.

"Yes!" Jamal says.

I shake the water out of my ears, glad I helped make the first point for our team. Jamal and Lenni splash over to me for a high-five. We slap palms gleefully. Beyond Lenni's head, I watch Darryl watching us. He hesitates, then smiles.

"Nice save," he says.

"Come on, you guys," Gaby hollers. "Serve!"

I turn around and get back in my position, across the imaginary net from Manny. I can't help grinning a little. Things aren't half bad after all. I have friends, I'm a writer. And for once, I don't want to be anyplace except where I am, hanging out on a sunny afternoon.

EPILOGUE

October 6

You're never going to believe the day I had today! It was so amazing, I thought I'd write about it while I'm waiting up.

Okay, first of all, today was the last day of school before the Columbus three-day weekend and Jason is coming home tonight! He's driving from school with a friend of his. They're arriving at midnight. I've already taken all my clothes off Jason's bed and put them away in the closet. I also cleaned the old soda cans and dirty socks off the floor. This is the cleanest this room has ever been, and I still have two hours to kill.

Anyway, the best news: I got home from school today and there was a letter for me from Planet X, *this magazine I wrote to back in September. They sent me a ten-dollar check and they're going to publish my "Peace Words" story!!!!!!!!!!!!!!!*

I was so excited, I ran out into the living room to show my parents, even though they don't know anything about what happened over the summer. Mom said she'd get me a frame for the letter so I can hang it up in my room. I'm going to make a copy of the check before I cash it so I can frame it with the letter!

Even Dad was nice to me, in his own weird way. He said he was proud of me for "following something through" and whapped me on the back.

I called a rally to get my friends together and they were hyped. Gaby kept saying, "Are we going to be famous?" I had to tell her like ten times that Planet X is this tiny magazine in Boston, so everyone in the world is not going to be reading my story.

Anyway, get this, Jamal was with me when I got the letter, and then he said he had to go get something and left. When he came back, he gave me a plastic bag. Inside was a sheet of stick-on earrings. The kind girls wear when they're not allowed to get their ears pierced. Right in the middle between all these stars and hearts were two fake diamonds.

Jamal said, "Even if you're not being Diamond Jones all the time anymore, it was an important phase in your career." That made the whole team crack up. I taped the fake diamond studs on the front cover of this notebook, to remind me. Lenni, Tina, and Gaby divvied up the rest of the earrings.

To celebrate my first published story, I treated everybody to ice cream, Double Fudge and Very Berry, using up almost my whole October allowance. Two cartons of ice cream are almost as much as the money I just earned for my story!

Anyway, life is looking up. And speaking of ice cream, there's some left in the fridge and I think I'm going to have seconds before Jason and his friend get here and finish it off. He'll be home in one hour and forty-five minutes now!

Later!
Rob